CAPTURED!

You step inside the matter-transmitter booth, and a moment later you find yourself in a large glass case. Outside the case, bending over it, is a huge creature, twelve feet high at least.

"I've caught another one trying to transmit," the creature says in a deep, muffled voice.

"Another one!" says an even deeper voice. A second creature stares at you through the glass. "You'd better let it go before we get into trouble," it says.

"But I just caught it!" the first one protests.

The two creatures continue to argue. Finally, the smaller one opens the top of the glass case. Its huge tentacle reaches in and wraps itself around your body!

D1598110

Bantam Books in the Escape™ from Tenopia series
Ask your bookseller for the books you have missed

FROM TENOPIA
#4

STAR SYSTEM TENOPIA

by Richard Brightfield

Created by Edward Packard

Illustrated by David Perry

BANTAM BOOKS
TORONTO · NEW YORK · LONDON · SYDNEY · AUCKLAND

RL 5, IL age 10 and up

STAR SYSTEM TENOPIA
A Bantam Book / September 1986

Escape is a trademark of Metabooks, Inc.

ISBN 0-553-25637-8

Published simultaneously in the United States and Canada

Bantam Books are published by Bantam Books, Inc. Its trade-
mark, consisting of the words "Bantam Books" and the por-
trayal of a rooster, is Registered in U.S. Patent and Trademark
Office and in other countries. Marca Registrada. Bantam
Books, Inc., 666 Fifth Avenue, New York, New York 10103.

STAR SYSTEM TENOPIA

NOTICE!!!

You are about to find yourself trapped in the most forbidding star system in the galaxy: Star System Tenopia. It's important that you follow the directions in this book if you hope to escape!

During your travels through the star system, you'll have a small computer that can project a map of any planet you wish to see. To use this, flip to the map page indicated near the bottom of the page you're reading. (When you turn to a map page, be sure to keep a finger on the page you're reading so you won't lose your place.)

Whether or not you escape from Star System Tenopia will depend on how skillful you are, how persistent you are, and how lucky you are. Will you succeed— or will you be trapped forever? It's entirely up to you!

You're on the navigation deck of a galactic patrol starship heading through Star System Tenopia on your way home to Earth. On a wide screen above the navigator's console you can see the planet Tenopia shrinking into an ever-smaller ball as you leave it far behind.

A diplomat from Earth, you were traveling through Star System Tenopia on your way to the Mylaean cluster when your own ship was hit by a meteor. You crash-landed on Tenopia, the nearest planet, and after many adventures managed to locate the galactic patrol base. There you boarded the galactic patrol starship and embarked into space.

Jarn, the ship's navigator, is seated next to you in front of the large console. He flips one of the switches, and the view of Tenopia on the screen is replaced by a diagram of the whole planetary system. Star System Tenopia contains eleven planets which revolve around a large orange sun.

"Here's the relative position of the planets," says Jarn. "Of course, the scale here is inaccurate. Each planet is between fifty and one hundred million miles away from the next closest planet. Two of the planets—Valug and Tarnor—are gas giants. They're completely uninhabitable."

As you look at the diagram of Star System Tenopia, Jarn begins to tell you about each planet.

Go on to the next page.

THE TENOPIAN
STAR SYSTEM

Turn to page 4.

4

"There's Sondar," Jarn is saying. "The Sondarians have always helped the galactic patrol—"

Jarn stops talking as sirens suddenly start blaring all over the starship. "That alarm is only used when the ship is under attack!" he exclaims. "Wait here! I've got to report to my emergency station."

Jarn runs off. Seconds later, a sharp jolt knocks you off your chair and onto the floor. The navigation screen goes blank, and the main lights go out, to be replaced a few seconds later by dim emergency lights. You are picking yourself up when Jarn returns to the navigation deck.

"The Maglan pirates have attacked the ship," he says tensely. "They've knocked out our primary defense and communication systems. And they're towing us somewhere with a tractor beam."

"Isn't there anything we can do?" you ask.

"Not much for now," Jarn replies. "There's no use trying to get away in an escape pod. The pirates would pick us off in a second. There's only one thing I can think of: there's a maintenance crawl space behind the navigation console. The electronic circuits of the console will block any bioscan. When the ship lands, we can hide in there."

Turn to page 8.

You head out through space. The orange sun hangs like a huge rubber ball against a background of black velvet sprinkled with a myriad of stars.

Suddenly, you notice a streak of light coming toward you. You head away from it, but as you soon learn, it's a pirate spaceship. Your small craft is no match for its speed or for the powerful tractor beam that shoots out across space and traps your scoutcraft in its rays.

In minutes your ship is drawn aboard the pirate craft. You're taken prisoner and locked in a small cell. As the guards walk away, one says, "We'll add this scoutcraft we just captured to our fleet on Tenopia. We'll be there soon."

Turn to page 29.

6

"That craft looks operational," Jarn whispers. "If we can get aboard, we may be able to escape before the pirates detect us.

"Our only hope for returning to Earth is to find the emergency galactic patrol starship located somewhere in the Tenopian star system."

"You're a member of the galactic patrol," you say. "Don't you know where it is?"

"Unfortunately not," he replies. "Only the highest-ranking members of the patrol are given its exact location. With all of the warring factions in this star system, it's too much of a risk for the entire patrol to have that kind of information. But we *are* given a key to it. Should we ever reach the starship, it will respond to this key and a spoken code." He takes out a small, thin circle of metal and shows it to you. It bears the raised imprint of a pelephin, an intelligent dolphinlike creature found on Tenopia.

"I don't suppose they told you what the code is," you say.

"No," Jarn answers. "I do know that it consists of five words, and that five of the Sondarian research stations located throughout Star System Tenopia have each been given one of those words. We'll have to piece it together."

You and Jarn creep toward the scoutcraft. Jarn suddenly pulls you down.

Turn to page 9.

"I wish I knew where they're taking us," Jarn says. "With the navigational equipment out of action, we're—"

"I have my pocket computer," you interrupt. "I'll set it on its planetary mode. That will automatically display a detailed map of the closest planet within the star system relative to my position in space. But I can call up a map of any other planet just by keyboarding the name of the planet I want to see."

"That computer has quite a range," says Jarn. "Does it estimate the distance to each planet as well?"

"No, I'll have to rely on navigational equipment for that."

Hours later, as your ship enters the atmosphere of a planet, Jarn asks, "Which planet are we approaching now?"

Turn to page 15.

"There's a guard by the door," Jarn says in a low whisper. "I'll go first and try to jump him. You stay close behind."

Jarn almost pulls it off, but as he grapples with the guard, the noise alerts some of the other guards not far away. Whistles and the sound of running feet come at you from all directions.

"Escape *now!*" Jarn shouts, and at the same time manages to toss you the small disk—the key to the galactic patrol starship. "And that's an order!"

Turn to page 17.

"I've escaped from the Maglan pirates, and I'm looking for a way to get back to Earth," you say.

"Very well," the voice says. "Approach the tower."

As you near the tower you have a funny feeling in your head. Finally, a door opens and a woman with pointed ears, dressed in a white lab coat, is standing there.

"Your story checks out with what I can read in your mind," she says. "I am sorry that I damaged your craft, but it will be repaired. You approached so suddenly, and . . ."

"Excuse me," you interrupt, "but there's something I have to ask you."

Go on to the next page.

"Yes," the Sondarian woman says, "you want to know if I can give you part of the code. I will give you one word, and that is *arcs*.

"Now, please leave. I have much work to do. A repair robot has fixed your scoutcraft."

You thank her for her help and climb inside the scoutcraft. Before you leave Samelbub, you want to search for the galactic patrol starship.

 TO CHECK MAP OF SAMELBUB, TURN TO PAGE 19.

If you head toward the grasslands,
turn to page 72.

If you head toward the fern forest, turn to page 89.

Crowds of strange creatures are pouring from the parking lot into the festival grounds. You have no Veendian currency, but, luckily, you're able to attach yourself to a group of hominids that resemble humans closely, and you enter along with them.

There are booths offering different kinds of food from all parts of Star System Tenopia. Some make you shudder to look at them; others would be welcomed at any dinner table back on Earth. Over one of the booths is a sign with a drawing of what could be a starship. Excitedly you run over to the booth and ask what the drawing is.

"That's a picture of a Bazulian interplanetary ship," says the creature in the booth.

You must look disappointed because the creature asks, "What did you hope it was?"

"I thought it might be a picture of a starship. I'm looking for one to get back to my own planet, Earth," you say.

"Ah! I see," says the creature. "I've heard talk of just such a starship on my own planet, Bazul. Perhaps you should go there. If you don't find anything there, you could try asking on Sondar."

Go on to the next page.

Sondar! you think. All roads, or at least spaceways, seem to lead to Sondar. Do the Sondarians actually know where the starship is? you wonder.

TO CHECK MAP OF SONDAR, SEE PAGE 77.

TO CHECK MAP OF BAZUL, SEE PAGE 101.

If you decide to go directly to Sondar, turn to page 88.

If you decide to go to Bazul first, turn to page 58.

You take the small map computer out of your pocket and show it to Jarn. On the computer screen is the map of a planet that looks something like Earth.

"Samelbub!" Jarn says. "It's a planet in the same stage of geological evolution as prehistoric Earth. The pirates must have a base there!"

The starship lands, and you and Jarn hide in the crawl space behind the navigation console. The pirates swarm aboard, quickly squelching any resistance. They search the ship with scanners, looking for life-forms. But the elaborate wiring of the navigation console blocks the electrical waves that you and Jarn, like all life-forms, emit. The pirates take the rest of the crew prisoner and move the starship to a large storage hangar.

Soon all is quiet outside the ship. You and Jarn sneak out an emergency exit beneath the starship. The hangar is dark, but a column of starlight streams through a tall crack where one of the hangar doors is not completely closed. Carefully, you and Jarn work your way through the shadowy hangar over to the door. You look outside. Not far away a small scoutcraft is parked.

Turn to page 6.

16

From your previous trip here, you know that your control system will blank out if you stay in the tower's energy field. You remember the code word that the Sondarian woman gave you: *arcs*. Deciding that you've gotten all the information from Samelbub that you're likely to need, you quickly check your fuel supply. You're sure you can reach either Alkon or Feenar from here.

TO CHECK MAP OF ALKON, SEE PAGE 49.

TO CHECK MAP OF FEENAR, SEE PAGE 39.

If you decide to visit Alkon, turn to page 48.

If you decide to visit Feenar instead, turn to page 34.

You jump aboard the scoutcraft and dash into the cockpit. You hate to leave Jarn behind, but you know that if you can find the hidden starship, you can help Jarn and the entire crew.

Quickly you press the takeoff and acceleration buttons. The scoutcraft soars into the air and streaks away at top speed. In seconds, you leave the pirate base far behind, but the pirates will be after you soon. You have to make a decision—and fast.

You check your map computer. Few place names are given on your map of Samelbub. You know you want to stay away from Drakon, the Maglan pirate base. The Valley of the Dinosaurs and the tar pits also look like places to avoid. The fern forest might be a good place to hide. On the other hand, the Sondarian research station might be one of the stations that has been given part of the code you'll need to get back to Earth.

 TO CHECK MAP OF SAMELBUB, SEE PAGE 19.

If you land in the fern forest, turn to page 89.

If you head toward the research station, turn to page 26.

VOLCANOES

FERN FOREST

VOLCANOES

VALLEY OF THE DINOSAURS

MOUNTAINS

SAMELBUB

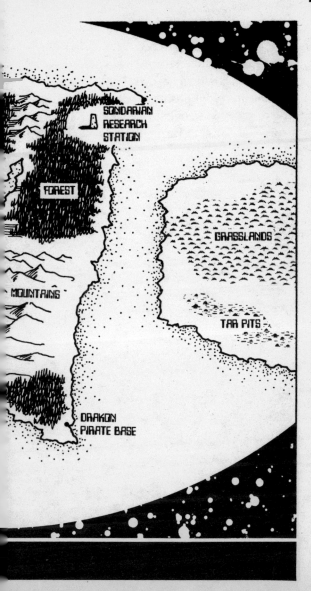

You wait in your cell, knowing that you can get out through the porthole under cover of darkness. But you have to wait for several days before you see a deserted scoutcraft parked near your cell. That night, you slip away from your prison and dash to the scoutcraft. You make it safely, but the ship is short on fuel. You're forced to travel to Bazul, the nearest planet.

Turn to page 58.

The Sondarian eyes you carefully. At last he says, "Very well, Earthling. It seems you speak the truth. The code word this station has been given is *over*. Perhaps my superiors on Sondar can tell you more about the location of the starship."

"But—"

The Sondarian cuts you off. "If you have all five code words, then I am authorized to give you a scout-craft to seek the Council of Elders on Sondar. They will find out soon enough if you truly know the secret code. If you do not have the words, I suggest you enter the matter transmitter. Perhaps the computer on OS–2 could provide you with more of the information you seek."

If you know all five code words, turn to page 32.

If you don't have all the code words, enter the matter transmitter and turn to page 40.

"My friend here *escaped* from the pirates," Hrar says loudly, "and is looking for a way to get back to the planet Earth."

A murmur goes through the café.

Leading you toward a booth, Hrar continues to address the crowd. "Go on about your business, all of you, unless you have some information about where my friend can find a starship to return to Earth."

All around the café conversations begin again. When the sound level is almost back to normal—loud—a very tall, very thin creature slides into the booth alongside Hrar.

"Ah, Tslin, my friend," Hrar says, "It's good to see you."

"I'm interested in your companion's escape from the pirates," Tslin says.

You tell him the whole story of your travels in Star System Tenopia.

"All of us here live in fear of pirates," Tslin says. "Earth's base of the galactic patrol is much stronger than ours. If you can get back to Earth and alert them to our plight, it might help. Unfortunately, we don't know where the starship is hidden, but we'll see to it that your scoutcraft is refueled and reprovisioned before you start off again on your search. Perhaps the people of Dyal—Mazar's other city—can help you."

You thank Tslin for his help and leave with Hrar. When you return to your scoutcraft, you are met there by several Mang who are already working on the ship. You decide your next stop will be Dyal.

TO CHECK MAP OF MAZAR, SEE PAGE 61.

Turn to page 46.

"You have not acquired the code!" the Sondarian elder thunders at you. "You dare to approach the Council of Elders without complete and accurate information! Go, and come back only when you are sure that you speak the truth!"

Tanalia leads you back toward the scoutcraft. "What should I do now?" you ask her, your spirits drooping.

"You must visit the planets that have Sondarian research stations to collect the code words that you need," she tells you kindly. "You may have thought you had all five words, but you were wrong. Listen closely when you hear each code word—and when you have all five, head for the planet of OS–2 as quickly as you can. The robot there will be programmed to let us know when you are ready to return."

You thank Tanalia and climb into your scoutcraft.

Turn to page 5.

As your scoutcraft approaches the Sondarian research station on Samelbub, you see a high, cylindrical tower rising out of a forest. When you get closer, you see flashes from the top of the tower. Then sudden air-bursts all around your scoutcraft make it bounce violently.

If you've visited the Sondarian Research Station on Samelbub before, turn to page 16. If not, read on . . .

The power in your ship fails. The controls stop working. The scoutcraft crashes through the trees and comes to a jarring stop about a mile away from the tower. So much for the research station, you think as you climb out of the ship's escape hatch and drop to the ground. You keyboard the command to switch your map computer out of its planetary mode so you can see a detailed map of your precise location. The map of the planet Samelbub remains on the computer screen. Your computer's stuck in its planetary mode! Just then you hear a woman's voice booming through the forest. "Identify yourself and state your reason for approaching the tower," it demands.

Turn to page 10.

Tlar is a neatly laid out city of broad streets.

If you've visited Tlar before, turn to page 44. If not, read on . . .

As you walk down one street you see a museum, a library, a laboratory, and a university. In the center of the city is a large traveler's information building where you learn, to your surprise, that there is a Sondarian research station on Bazul's other side.

"But it's not on my map!" you say.

"Only the Sondarians can stand the heat on the hot side," says the Bazulian at the information desk, shrugging. "I don't advise you to visit there. It's a fiery wasteland."

"Would I be *permitted* to travel there?" you inquire, explaining that you are a diplomat from Earth.

"I could find out." She places a call to the embassy.

"The embassy doesn't want you to try it," she reports. "Here's my advice: slip into their transmitter when nobody's looking and set the dial to three."

"Thanks!" You hurry to the embassy.

Turn to page 125.

Through a porthole in your cell, you see the familiar landscape of Tenopia far below you. There's Tenopia Island and there, the continent of Kabran.

If you've been imprisoned in the Maglan pirate base on Tenopia before, turn to page 20. If not, read on . . .

The pirate ship lands at its base on Kabran. The pirates just leave you in your cell and go about their business. Soon all is quiet in the corridor outside the cell. Through the porthole you can see that the ship is parked in the middle of a wide field. Night has fallen on Tenopia, but there is a dim light from the windows of a building across the field.

On a hunch, you try to release the safety latch on the porthole. It works! The thick glass window opens inward. You manage to squeeze through and drop down to the ground. All of the pirates seem to be in the building across the field. Between you and the building is a scoutcraft, not unlike the one you were captured in. You wonder if you should try to get to the scoutcraft or slip into the woods on the other side of the large parked spaceship you just climbed out of.

If you head for the scoutcraft, turn to page 33.

If you head for the woods, turn to page 107.

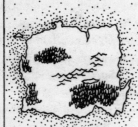

SEA KINGDOM
OF SALERIA

SALERIAN
ISLANDS

TENOPIA
ISLAND

TENOPIA

KABRAN

MAGLAN
PIRATE
BASE

"As you have acquired the code," the Sondarian says, "you may proceed to the town of Varavam on Sondar. The Council of Elders is waiting for you there."

**TO CHECK MAP OF SONDAR,
SEE PAGE 77.**

Turn to page 55.

Crouching low and moving as quietly as you can, you dash over to the scoutcraft. It's unlocked and un-occupied! You slip quietly inside and check out the controls.

Then you take off, wincing at the noise the space-craft makes. You know the pirates will be after you soon. Checking your navigation console, you see that you have just enough fuel to get to the planet Mazar.

You aim your scoutcraft toward Mazar and acceler-ate to as high a velocity as you can. Then you switch off all power on the ship. If there's a tracking device on the ship, you figure it's probably powered from the central power supply. It turns out that you're right, and you escape the pirates.

 **TO CHECK MAP OF MAZAR,
SEE PAGE 61.**

Turn to page 60.

You head for Feenar, the park planet of Star System Tenopia, and land in a parking lot for spaceships near the city of Veend.

If you've been to Veend before, turn to page 113. If not, read on . . .

There are hundreds of different kinds of spaceships in the lot, but all of them are for interplanetary travel. You see no starships, the kind needed to reach other star systems—the kind that you need to get back to Earth.

A family of tentacled creatures is just getting out of their medium-sized spaceship. As you walk toward them the largest creatures emit high-pitched shrieks of alarm. The young ones dash off to hide behind a clump of nearby trees. You suddenly realize that they're terrified by the sight of you. You don't go any closer, but you call out to them that you're a friend.

Turn to page 37.

Hrar leads you through one of the narrow alleys between the buildings to a small, square door that opens into a rickety elevator. You and Hrar step inside, and it begins to descend by fits and starts.

The elevator finally gets down to the twentieth level. You step out and find yourself in a wide, dimly lit corridor. Here and there on the floor are large pools of water, and the sides of the corridor are lined with once-fine shops that are now boarded up.

"This way," Hrar says.

You follow him down to the end of the corridor and then left into another, zigzagging for some time through a maze of corridors. You begin to hear a hubbub of noise in the distance—humanlike laughter and the squeaks and whistles of nonhominid races. As you round a corner, you see the entrance to a café. Hrar ushers you inside.

A few heads turn as you enter, but most of the inhabitants just ignore you. Some of them make Hrar look almost human by comparison; others could pass for humans if it weren't for some obvious differences like tails or antennae.

"I sure hope there aren't any pirates in here," you whisper to Hrar.

Suddenly, the whole place becomes deathly quiet. All heads—some on two-headed creatures—turn to look at you.

Turn to page 23.

"I'm looking for a starship and a place to refuel my scoutcraft," you explain.

One of the creatures comes cautiously toward you—but is careful not to get too close. "I don't know about a starship," it says, "but we'll be glad to give you some fuel if you'll go away and leave us alone."

Following the creature's directions, you move your smaller ship up to the side of theirs. A long tube comes out of the larger ship and transfers fuel to yours.

"Thanks for the fuel," you say. "I'll leave right away."

"You might try the annual festival at Veend. It's going on right now," says the creature. "There'll be creatures from all over the star system there."

 TO CHECK MAP OF FEENAR, SEE PAGE 39.

Turn to page 13.

GRASSLANDS

SONDARIAN
RESEARCH
STATION

CENTRAL
LAKE

GARDENS &
GUEST HOUSES

SOUTH SEA

FEENAA

You arrive inside an airlock on the artificial planet, OS–2.

If you've been to OS–2 before, turn to page 50. If not, read on . . .

The first thing you do is check your computer map.

The entire surface of OS–2 is covered with a smooth metal shell. The entrance is a large rectangular hole in the surface, wide enough to admit a spacecraft. The center of the planet is hollow, except for an artificial sun suspended from the inner ring of structures that form the city of OS–2. A central computer is housed in one of the structures.

A panel slides open in a side wall of the airlock, and a small robot wheels out.

"My sensors tell me that you are not a robot, and are in fact an oxygen-breathing life-form," the robot says in a mechanical voice.

"That's right," you say. "I'm a diplomat from the planet Earth and I'm looking for a disguised or hidden starship that can take me back there."

"There is nothing hidden or disguised on OS–2, that I can assure you," says the robot. "But let us run your problem through the central computer. Follow me!"

Turn to page 42.

You hover over the egg for a few more minutes, but you hear no thought exchange in your mind. And there's no sign of the young Sondarian you saw here before. You can remember the code word that he gave you: *pelephin*.

At last you decide to give up on Mazar for the time being. Checking your fuel gauge, you estimate that you could reach one of four planets from here: Alkon, the desert planet; Bazul, the planet with a hot and cold side; Samelbub, the prehistoric planet, and Tenopia, the most treacherous planet in the star system.

TO CHECK MAP OF ALKON, SEE PAGE 49.

TO CHECK MAP OF BAZUL, SEE PAGE 101.

TO CHECK MAP OF TENOPIA, SEE PAGE 31.

TO CHECK MAP OF SAMELBUB, SEE PAGE 19.

If you make the short hop to Bazul, turn to page 58.

If you decide to visit Alkon, turn to page 48.

If you brave the dangers of Samelbub, turn to page 26.

If you dare to visit Tenopia, turn to page 5.

The robot leads you to an elevator that goes down into the complex—or is it up? you wonder. You reach a broad, high-arched passageway that stretches into the distance in both directions. An open trolley runs on tracks down the center. The trolley stops just long enough for you and the robot to get on. Then it starts off again and zips down the corridor.

TO CHECK MAP OF OS–2, SEE NEXT PAGE.

Turn to page 69.

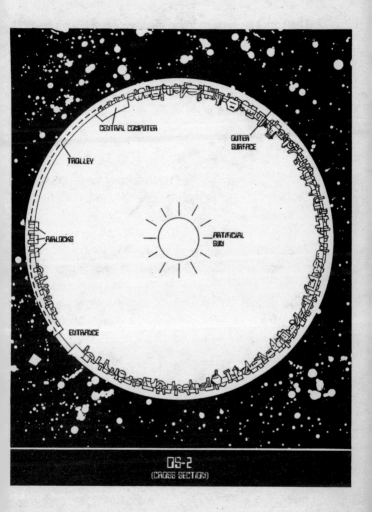

CENTRAL COMPUTER

OUTER
SURFACE

TROLLEY

AIRLOCKS

ARTIFICIAL
SUN

ENTRANCE

OS-2
(CROSS SECTION)

Back in Tlar, you visit the museum, the library, the laboratory, and the university, but you learn nothing new about the galactic starship's location. At last you walk to the embassy, where the matter transmitter is housed. Before stepping inside, you study the directions on the controls:

To OS–2: dial 1

To SONDAR: dial 2

The third choice—to travel to the Sondarian research station on Bazul's other side—no longer exists.

"Too dangerous" is the only explanation your embassy guide will offer. "Please enter the transmitter now. You're holding up the line."

TO CHECK MAP OF OS–2, SEE PAGE 43.

TO CHECK MAP OF SONDAR, SEE PAGE 77.

If you set the dial to 1, turn to page 40.

If you set the dial to 2, turn to page 74.

You take off in your scoutcraft. When you reach the boundary between the hot and cold sides of Bazul, you skim along the surface in the ship, searching for anything that might indicate a hidden starship. There's no sign of anything unusual on the surface of the planet, but you notice that something in your pocket is getting very warm. It's the key to the starship that Jarn gave you during your escape from the pirates.

You take it out and hold it gingerly in the palm of your hand. This may mean that I'm getting close, you think. Then up ahead, you see what looks like a tower rising right at the dividing line between the two sides of the planet. As you get closer you realize that it could be . . . It is! It's a starship, its nose pointed to the heavens.

Your scoutcraft circles, and then its extendable airlock clamps onto the port at the base of the larger ship. Eagerly, you climb out of your ship.

Turn to page 51.

You skim over the ocean in your scoutcraft, now refueled and tuned-up, enjoying the way it handles. Soon, up ahead, you see another floating city. According to your computer map, this is Dyal. Nearing the city, you see that it's smaller and less prosperous looking than Aquar. You wonder how many levels, if any, it has below the water. The layout is roughly the same as Aquar, though on a smaller scale.

You land in the central plaza and get out of your ship to look around. A Mang is curled up on a bench on one side of the plaza. It appears to be sleeping as you walk over to it.

"Hello!" you say loudly.

The creature opens one of its eyes. The other two remain tightly closed.

"I'm trying to get some information," you say, deciding that this Mang is probably trustworthy like Hrar. "Some information about a hidden starship."

All three of the Mang's eyes open wide.

"Not long ago, some of the Maglan pirates stopped here," it says. "They caused all sorts of trouble before they left. But I overheard them talking about just such a starship. They were looking for it themselves."

Go on to the next page.

"Did they know where it is?" you ask.

"Not really," the Mang answers. "They seemed to think it was either on Sondar or Feenar, and they were going to try Sondar first. If you want my advice, I'd avoid Sondar until I was sure that crew had left. All they have to do is see your scoutcraft and you can consider yourself a Maglan prisoner. Feenar would be a safe bet; the park rangers protect its inhabitants well. Of course, there are other ways to travel. Try the Sondarian research station on this planet. Maybe they'll send you by matter transmission."

**TO CHECK MAP OF MAZAR,
SEE PAGE 61.**

**TO CHECK MAP OF FEENAR,
SEE PAGE 39.**

*If you go to the Sondarian Research Station,
turn to page 127.*

If you go to Feenar, turn to page 34.

You enter Alkon's thin, hot atmosphere and search the desert surface below for landmarks.

If you've been to Narnk before, turn to page 68. If not, read on . . .

According to your map computer, Alkon is inhabited only on one side. When you can't make out anything below, you wonder if you're landing on the uninhabited side. Then you see a faint circular outline on the ground. That could indicate an underground settlement, you think. You land your scoutcraft near the circle and get out to investigate.

Suddenly a deep rumbling comes from the center of the circle, and a geyser of sand shoots into the air. A cylindrical structure pushes out of the sand, and you see a door at ground level. A mechanical-sounding voice says in the galactic tongue, "Enter if you wish, but leave all of your weapons behind."

You don't have any weapons, so that's no problem. But it could be a trap!

TO CHECK MAP OF ALKON, SEE NEXT PAGE.

Turn to page 78.

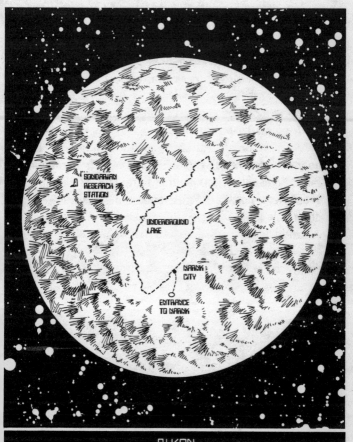

ALKON
(INHABITED SIDE)

The sliding panel in the airlock's side wall opens, and the robot who greeted you on your last trip to OS–2 wheels toward you. You can see its sensors registering your presence.

"You have visited us before, and we cannot help you any further," the robot says.

"Where do you suggest I go?" you ask. "I'm traveling by matter transmitter."

"As a diplomat, you are entitled to use one of our scoutcraft for as long as you need it," the robot replies. "But before you go anywhere, I have been programmed to ask you this: Have you acquired the code?"

If you're sure you know all five code words, turn to page 90.

If not, turn to page 105.

Suddenly, a deep voice calls, "Halt!" Two officers of the galactic patrol have entered your airlock and have laser guns aimed at you. One demands an explanation of your presence, while the other begins methodically to search you.

You're telling them about Jarn when the first officer says, "Jarn escaped from the pirates, and he did let us know you'd be searching for the ship."

At that moment the other officer takes the still-warm key from your pocket. "Looks like Jarn's friend, all right," he says, and then turns to you. "If you've got the correct code, then you've earned the right to use the ship." He hands you back the key.

Go on to the next page.

52

Your heart pounds as you approach the starship. You hold the key against a circular panel in the door. Immediately, there is a whirring sound from inside the ship. Slowly the door slides open. You go in, and the door closes behind you.

Turn to page 123.

You walk through endless rolling grasslands. After several hours you see a huge metallic tube in the distance.

If you've visited the Sondarian Research Station on Feenar before, turn to page 63. If not, read on . . .

You run toward the tube, hoping it's the starship. But you soon realize that the tube is actually a tower. As you circle its base a silver door glides open, and a tall hominid invites you in.

"Welcome to the Sondarian research station on Feenar," he says. "We have outposts throughout Star System Tenopia to observe the inhabitants and customs of each planet. You do not look like a native of Feenar."

"No," you say. "I'm from Earth, and I'm trying to find the galactic patrol starship that will take me back there."

"You will not find it on Feenar," the Sondarian says. He offers no further information.

Wondering if he's testing you, you hold out the silver disk. "This was given to me by Jarn, a navigator in the galactic patrol," you say. "He's been captured by the Maglan pirates."

Turn to page 21.

As you spiral down into the atmosphere of Sondar you are struck by the planet's similarity to Earth—the same blue oceans and broad expanses of green. There's even a similar scattering of white clouds just above the surface.

You check your computer map and head toward Varavam.

As you get out of your ship a lone figure in a silvery robe walks toward you.

If you've stood before the Council of Elders in Varavam before, turn to page 65. If not, read on . . .

You can see that it's a female with long, blond hair. If it weren't for her pointed ears, she could easily pass for human. "My name is Tanalia," she calls out in a high, musical voice. "May I be of assistance?"

"Perhaps," you say. "I'm looking for the Council of Elders."

Tanalia shrugs. "Many seek the elders but do not find them."

"Probably not," you say. "But I've acquired a code that I'll need to activate a galactic patrol starship hidden somewhere in the Tenopian star system. I've been told the elders are waiting for me."

"Yes," she says. "I believe the Council of Elders can help you. Follow me."

Turn to page 65.

56

You arrive at the city of Torc on the dark side of the planet Bazul.

If you've been to Torc before, turn to page 100. If not, read on . . .

Almost all of the city of Torc is devoted to making and growing things. Heat from the hot side of Bazul is collected and used to generate electricity, which is sent to cities all over the dark, cold side. The electricity is also pumped into large greenhouses in Torc itself. There, under artificial light, large quantities of food are grown. Automated factories fill another whole section of the city. You see all sorts of vehicles hauling raw materials and finished products.

Bazulians are hominids, resembling humans in most ways, except for their oddly shaped heads. The few that you see seem very busy. You have a hard time finding one who will stop and talk about what you're looking for. In addition, you have to shout over the sound of all the machinery around you.

Turn to page 62.

As you speed toward Bazul you remember what you know about it. You know that it has an unusual rotation—one side is always turned toward Tenopia's orange sun. On that side the temperatures are in the hundreds of degrees. The other side is always dark and cold, and that's where all of the settlements are. Special tunnels collect superheated gasses from the hot side and bring them to the cold side, where they are stored and used to generate electricity throughout the inhabited side of the planet.

Trying to decide where you'll land, you circle about 1,000 feet above the planet. Its cratered surface reminds you of Earth's moon, and suddenly you feel very homesick. You shrug off the feeling and set your navigation controls for Tlar, one of Bazul's two cities.

TO CHECK MAP OF BAZUL, SEE PAGE 101.

Turn to page 28.

You search thoroughly, but you don't find the hidden starship of the galactic patrol. At last you turn back toward the town of Varavam on Sondar.

Turn to page 122.

60

Mazar looms ahead of you, a shimmering ball of blue.

If you've been to the city of Aquar before, turn to page 104. If not, read on . . .

At first, the sweep of the ocean seems unbroken by any land masses. You check your computer map; it shows several sites, all located on one side of the planet.

As you get closer, you see a few small dots on the ocean whose locations correspond to the sites on your map. One of them, Aquar, is directly below as you enter the atmosphere of Mazar. Your ship streaks down toward a huge, perfectly circular platform floating on the surface of the ocean. The top of the platform, which is about two miles in diameter, is laid out like a city; rectangular buildings line the sides of boulevards that radiate from the center. You land at the edge of a plaza in the center of the artificial island.

 TO CHECK MAP OF MAZAR, SEE NEXT PAGE.

Turn to page 66.

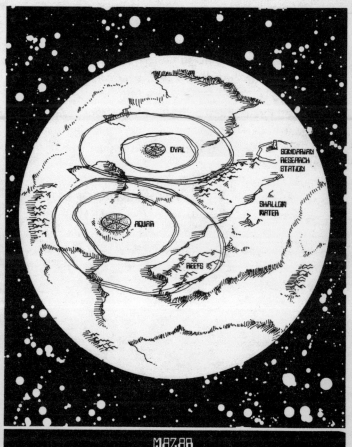

MAZAA
(INHABITED SIDE)

"I've heard rumors about a galactic patrol starship somewhere on Bazul," says the hominid you finally get to talk. "But I don't know where it could be. Perhaps up north. You might have an easier time getting information in the city of Tlar. It's the center of learning on Bazul."

"Can I travel there by matter transmitter?" you ask eagerly.

"Yes, certainly" is the welcome answer.

TO CHECK MAP OF BAZUL, SEE PAGE 101.

Turn to page 28.

As you approach the metallic tube, the silver door at its base opens. You enter expecting to see the tall Sondarian who greeted you on your first visit. But the room is empty, except for the small matter transmitter.

As you wait for someone to come and greet you, you remember the code word you were given on your earlier visit to this research station: *over*. You wait for an hour, but no one comes into the room. Since it doesn't seem like you'll learn anything else of value here, you decide to enter the matter transmitter.

Turn to page 40.

Tanalia leads you into a small whitewashed cottage. Inside, you find a large room dominated by a red oval table. Seven obviously aged Sondarians sit around it.

Before Tanalia can say a word, one of the elders leans forward. "What are the five code words?" he demands.

*If you say pelephin, glass, over, leaps, sea,
turn to page 25.*

*If you say arcs, glass, pelephin, liquid, over,
turn to page 114.*

*If you say liquid, pelephin, arcs, sea, over,
turn to page 91.*

You walk down one of the boulevards of Aquar, looking for someone to question. Most of the buildings look like warehouses or small factories of some sort, and you don't see anybody on the street. Then you hear a whisper from behind one of the buildings: "Hey! Earthling!"

You look into an alley to see who's talking and then jump back in fright. Next to the building is a large creature with many long spindly legs and three enormous eyes at the ends of stalks.

"Don't be alarmed, Earthling," it says. "*Your* body structure's as repulsive to me, a Mang, as a Chirconian slug!"

"How do you know that I'm from Earth?" you ask.

"We're not ignorant here on Aquar," says the creature. "I, Hrar, have my merchant's license in the second degree."

"Do you know anything about a hidden galactic starship?" you ask. "Ever since I escaped from the space pirates, I've been searching for it so that I can get back home."

Go on to the next page.

"A hidden starship's what you're looking for?" Hrar says. "That shouldn't be too hard to find. I'll take you down to the twentieth level, where the space pilots from many different planets gather. If they don't know where this starship of yours is, then nobody will."

"You mean twenty levels down under the water?" you ask.

"The neighborhood's a bit seedy, I'll have to admit," Hrar says.

Turn to page 36.

68

You fly south over the Alkonian desert, searching for any sign of the galactic patrol starship. Then, up ahead, you see a huge, dark cloud coming toward you. Quickly, you gain altitude and fly above it. A tremendous sandstorm is raging across the desert floor. You know that there's no chance you'll sight the starship through swirling sands below.

You check your fuel gauge—you have exactly enough to reach Feenar. On the other hand, it might make more sense to visit the Sondarian research station here on Alkon. If nothing else, you might be able to refuel there.

TO CHECK MAP OF ALKON,
SEE PAGE 49.

TO CHECK MAP OF FEENAR,
SEE PAGE 39.

*If you go to the Sondarian Research Station,
turn to page 128.*

If you go to Feenar, turn to page 34.

All along the route, you see crowds of robots mingling with hominids, all coming and going on various errands.

"Why would a hominid choose to live on this artificial planet?" you ask.

"The hominids you see are programmers for the central computer," the robot explains. "Few others live here. The data processing crew also serves diplomatic functions, taking word of our findings to other planets."

Go on to the next page.

After a short ride, you reach a chamber that holds a number of computer terminals. The robot seats you at one and quickly logs you on to the central computer.

The words *What is your question?* appear on your screen.

Turn to page 73.

72

You are heading toward the grasslands when the ship suddenly stops responding to the controls. Though you try to steer a straight course, the ship turns in a wide arc, heading south toward the Maglan pirate base. You try everything you can think of to control the ship, but nothing does any good.

You realize with a shudder that there's a homing device built into the scoutcraft. There's nothing you can do now but sit helplessly while the ship returns to the pirate base.

Turn to page 85.

"I'm looking for a hidden starship that will take me back to the planet Earth," you keyboard.

Immediately the response appears: *The starship you seek is between fire and ice.*

"Great," you moan. "Now all I have to know is where *that* is."

"I am sorry you did not find your journey more helpful," the robot says. "It is rare that the computer fails to provide accurate information—and of course, when it does fail, the fault always lies with the programmer."

The robot leaves you with one of the programmers, a distinguished-looking hominid from Feenar. He informs you that your diplomatic status entitles you to free and unlimited use of a scoutcraft. You choose a scoutcraft equipped with extra fuel tanks. A few hours later, you leave the hollow planet and head for Klanton.

**TO CHECK MAP OF KLANTON,
SEE PAGE 81.**

Turn to page 80.

You arrive in a matter-transmitter booth in the town of Tamsung on Sondar.

If you've been to Tamsung before, turn to page 120. If not, read on . . .

Outside the booth a delegation of Sondarians is waiting for you. "Welcome to Tamsung," says their leader. "We have been expecting you. We received word of your search through the spy network your friend Jarn has organized from prison. He has asked us to help you in any way possible."

"Jarn said the Sondarians have been given the code words—" you begin.

"Our *research stations* have been given code words," the leader interrupts. "And only five of the stations; even we don't know which ones have the code words. I am afraid the galactic patrol has very tight security." He stops, and then says kindly, "Do not be discouraged. You will obviously have to visit most, if not all, of the planets in the star system in order to assemble the code and find the starship, but we will help you."

Another Sondarian speaks up. "We here on Sondar travel by matter transmitter, as you know, but your search may take you to primitive regions where transmission has not been established. We suggest that you use a small scoutcraft. Fortunately, we have one here left by an alien."

Go on to the next page.

They show you the scoutcraft, which has a sleek red surface. You would like to ask more questions, but the Sondarians hurry you onto the ship.

"It has a range without refueling that will allow you to reach three other planets from here: Tenopia; Mazar, the water planet; or the ice planet, Klanton," the leader says.

"I've seen enough of Tenopia. I have no desire to return there," you say as you check both Mazar and Klanton on your map computer. Mazar is mostly water; only two cities lie on its ocean surface. Klanton shows mostly caverns, mountains, and cities of ice.

TO CHECK MAP OF MAZAR, SEE PAGE 61.

TO CHECK MAP OF KLANTON, SEE PAGE 81.

If you decide to go to Mazar, turn to page 127.

If you decide to go to Klanton, turn to page 80.

POL▮

• GRAVEL CITY

MOUNTAINS

FOREST

• KORNIK

FARMS &
FIELDS

OCEAN

DESERT

• VARAVAM

SOU▮

SONDAR

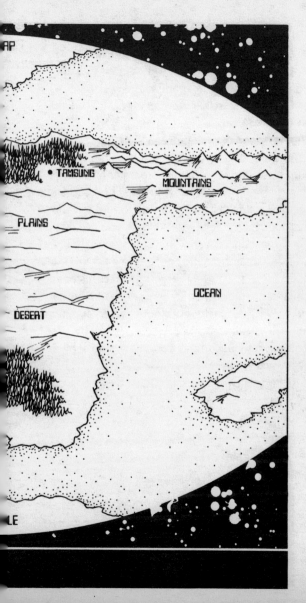

You step through the doorway of the cylinder. The door closes behind you, shutting you inside. Suddenly you're hurtling down. You're in an elevator—a fast one! Fortunately, it gradually slows down as it nears the bottom, so that you can hardly feel anything when it finally stops.

Another door opens and you step out. Ahead of you is a wide, brightly lit corridor. It seems to stretch straight as an arrow to infinity. You stand there for a minute, trying to decide what to do. Then you see a figure, tiny at that distance, coming toward you along the corridor. As the figure gets closer, you see that it's riding a mechanical cart. The cart stops in front of you, and a small hominid, not more than three feet high, jumps out. Though he's humanlike, his head is much larger in proportion to his body than a human's would be. His skin, where it's not covered by a tight-fitting suit of silvery material, is gray. His voice doesn't seem to be coming from his mouth at all, but you can hear it clearly nevertheless.

"My name is Dirn," he says. "Do you wish to go to Narnk?"

Go on to the next page.

"Narnk?" you repeat. "What is it?"

"It's the port of entry for the Federation of Alkon," Dirn says.

"I'm sorry I don't know more about where I am," you say. "I'm searching for a hidden starship to get me back to Earth."

"Well!" Dirn exclaims. "In that case, we should get to the laboratory at Narnk as quickly as possible. Jump on the back of this vehicle and we'll be off."

Turn to page 97.

80

As your ship spirals down toward Klanton, you don't see anything at first but ice, even though your map computer indicates that the city of Tantel should be somewhere below you.

If you've been to the city of Tantel before, turn to page 98. If not, read on . . .

Soon, a warning buzzer goes off on your navigation console. A star system directive is signaling for you to land. You guess that you're getting close to Tantel—the heat from your scoutcraft must present a threat to the ice city.

The outside air temperature reading is minus twenty when you land. You look in the ship's locker for something warm to wear. You find a light spacesuit that will do and put it on. Then you head out for the ice city that towers in the distance. As you reach the city limits a column of small, furry creatures, each with a single eyestalk rising from its head, comes out to meet you and lead you into the city.

Turn to page 82.

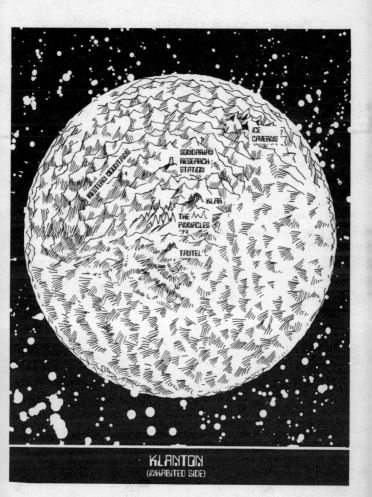

KLANTON
(INHABITED SIDE)

82

The inside of Tantel is a masterpiece of ice carving. The furry creatures lead you to a central council chamber. One of the creatures understands a bit of the galactic language. You explain, mostly with hand gestures, that you are looking for a starship of the galactic patrol. The interpreter *seems* to understand— you can't be sure. But you follow him when he leads you out of the city and over about a mile of frozen wasteland.

There, carved in ice down to the last detail, is a replica of a starship. You can only shake your head in disappointment. You thank the creature, anyway.

As you head back toward your scoutcraft, a large, saucer-shaped spaceship appears over the horizon and dives toward you. You try to jump out of the way, but slip on the ice. You tumble to the ground, cracking your head.

Turn to page 116.

Everything seems to blur for a second. It takes you a moment to realize that you are no longer on Sondar.

As you step out of your ship you see a man coming toward you. He is tall and fair like Tanalia, and has the same kind of pointed ears.

"I am Bertar," he says. "Tanalia has just sent me a message explaining what you are looking for. From my knowledge of Bazul, I know of two places that *I* would look.

"The unusual rotation of our planet keeps one side always facing the orange sun. We call that the hot side. There are tunnels carrying superheated gas from the hot side to various places on the cold side. And one place you should look for the starship is Torc, the junction point of the tunnels. The other place to look is the *boundary* between the hot side and the cold side."

**TO CHECK MAP OF BAZUL,
SEE PAGE 101.**

If you go to Torc, turn to page 59.

If you go to the boundary between the hot and cold sides of Bazul, turn to page 45.

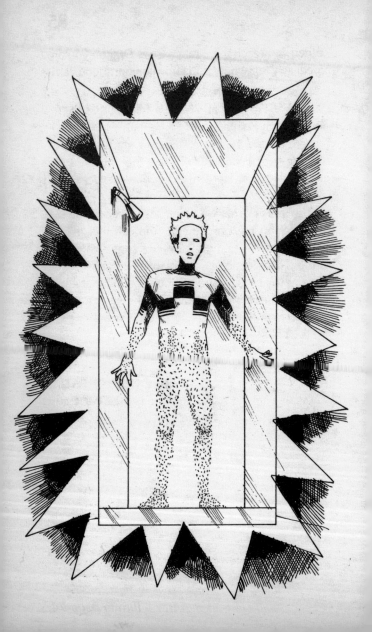

When you reach the pirate base at Drakon you are immediately thrown into prison with your friend Jarn.

If you've been imprisoned at Drakon before, turn to page 126. If not, read on . . .

Jarn has been plotting a method of escape with some captives from the planet Sondar. As a defense against the pirates, all Sondarians carry with them a small piece of a matter transmitter. So whenever a fairly large group of Sondarians is together, there's a good chance that they can assemble a working transmitter. Fortunately, enough Sondarians have been captured by the pirates to enable them to put a transmitter together. Jarn has helped them to assemble it and hide it inside a shower stall. They've decided to allow only one person a week to escape and hope that the disappearances won't be noticed. The pirates are too lazy to keep a careful account of all their prisoners.

Jarn has decided to stay in the prison and assist in sending more prisoners to safety. Because of your determination to find the galactic patrol starship, you're one of the first prisoners to be chosen for transmission.

On the day of your escape, you step into the "shower."

Turn to page 74.

You notice a group of figures in the doorway of the tall building. One of them beckons for you to come inside. You enter and find yourself in a huge laboratory. Tier after tier of equipment made of crystal and supported by structures of shiny metal rises up to a ceiling that must be a hundred feet over your head. A good deal of the equipment is in motion, and whirring and gurgling sounds fill the large room.

Noting your interest in their equipment, the Alkonians in the lab tell you they're scientists, studying the process of water conservation on their planet. You introduce yourself and explain that you're looking for a hidden starship—and trying to avoid the Maglan pirates. "Dirn brought me here from the surface," you add.

"Hmm! You're an interesting case," says one of the scientists. "My advice to you is to reclaim your scoutcraft and travel to Klanton, the ice planet."

"Why Klanton?" you ask.

Go on to the next page.

"We travel there frequently for water research," says the scientist. "It has a Sondarian research station. One of our scientists, Shind, is there. If you find her, she'll gladly act as interpreter for you with the Klantonians—the creatures of Klanton. You'd find her outside one of the two major cities, Klar or Tantel."

You decide to follow the scientist's advice and visit Klanton.

 TO CHECK MAP OF KLANTON, SEE PAGE 81.

If you travel to Klar, turn to page 118.

If you decide to visit Tantel, turn to page 80.

As you fly over the surface of Sondar you see dense forests and small, quaint villages that dot a carefully cultivated countryside. The scene reminds you of paintings of medieval times on Earth. Then you see a larger settlement below. Checking your computer map, you verify that the settlement is the village of Kornik.

If you've been to Kornik before, turn to page 121. If not, read on . . .

As you approach Kornik, you notice a small, sleek, egg-shaped building that looks out of place in the rural village. You land just outside the village. A friendly Sondarian comes out to meet you. When you ask him about the egg-shaped building, he explains that it contains a matter transmitter. "All the villages in Sondar have an *egg*," he says, smiling. "We use the matter transmitters to travel long distances. All local travel is by foot," he adds, "which keeps us healthy and the countryside unpolluted."

Turn to page 94.

You guide the scoutcraft to a landing in one of the few clearings that you can find in the fern forest. You've seen ferns in greenhouses back on Earth, but not like these! These must be fifty feet tall. You climb out of the scoutcraft and look around. The giant ferns tower over you, making you feel very small. This must be the way prehistoric Earth looked, you think, as you command your map computer to switch out of its planetary mode. You want to see a detailed map of your precise location, so you can plan your next move. The map of the planet Samelbub remains on the screen. Your computer's stuck in its planetary mode! Just then, you hear a distant noise. Curious, you wander from the ship.

Suddenly, the dense foliage comes alive as something thrashes toward you, roaring loudly. You dash back toward the scoutcraft. Behind you the roars grow louder—whatever the beast is, it's gaining on you.

Turn to page 92.

"Yes, I have the code," you tell the OS-2 robot.

It seems to bow, tilting its upper half toward you slightly. "Then you may proceed to the town of Varavam on Sondar. The Council of Elders awaits you there."

The robot leads you to a small hangar, where a sturdy scoutcraft equipped to carry extra fuel supplies is made ready for you.

Turn to page 55.

"That is incorrect!" the Sondarian elder screams. "Begone, and do not return until you speak the truth!"

You back out of the room quickly, followed by Tanalia. "But—" you stammer to her.

"Don't worry," she says soothingly. "Perhaps you thought you had all five words, but you were wrong. Here is what you must do now: visit as many of the planets as you must to collect the five code words. Listen closely when you hear each word—when you have all five, head for the planet of OS–2 as quickly as you can. The robot there will be programmed to let us know when you are ready to return."

"Thank you," you say gratefully. Then you consult your computer map. The planets closest to Sondar are Tenopia, Mazar, and Bazul.

 TO CHECK MAP OF TENOPIA, SEE PAGE 31.

TO CHECK MAP OF MAZAR, SEE PAGE 61.

TO CHECK MAP OF BAZUL, SEE PAGE 101.

If you travel to Tenopia next, turn to page 5.

If you visit Mazar instead, turn to page 60.

If your next choice is Bazul, turn to page 58.

You glance over your shoulder as you frantically race toward the ship. A huge lizard comes into view. One look at its razor-sharp teeth convinces you that this creature must be a relative of the tyrannosaur. It lumbers toward you, and with each step, the ground shakes violently.

You try hiding behind one of the ferns, but the dinosaur seems to sense your location. It's less than two strides away when you hear a loud whirring noise directly overhead. You look up—and see a Maglan pirate spaceship! Seconds later a tractor beam shoots down from the pirate ship and pulls you off the ground, into the air. Below you the dinosaur roars, snapping its enormous jaws at your retreating figure.

You're pulled into the underhatch of the pirate ship. The pirates tie you up and take you back to their base.

Turn to page 85.

You go into the village and ask around about the code and the starship. No one's heard of the code, but everyone seems to have heard of the starship, and everyone has a different opinion on its location. A lot of the townspeople are sure that it's on the planet Bazul—so sure, in fact, that you'd like to go there at once. But you don't have enough fuel in your scoutcraft to go directly to Bazul.

"Do you know where I can refuel?" you ask the crowd of Sondarians who have gathered around you.

"Not here—we do not use scoutcrafts," one answers.

"If you are willing to risk capture by the Maglan pirates, you might try to slip into their base on Tenopia."

It sounds like a risky idea, but you decide to chance it. Many hours later, you coast in toward the woods near the Maglan pirate base on Tenopia. You land quietly and work your way through a thick stretch of woods to the edge of a field. A dim light from a building across the field glows in the darkness.

Turn to page 107.

You land on the outskirts of Klar, hoping to find Shind or any other traveler who can provide you with a warm-suit. But nobody comes near your scoutcraft. After waiting a few hours, you decide to move on.

Checking your navigational equipment, you see several planets within fuel range: Tenopia, Samelbub, Feenar, and OS–2. Discarding Tenopia, the planet where you'll be in the greatest danger of capture by the Maglan pirates, you study the other three choices on your map computer. Feenar, the park planet, has a rest station where you can refuel. OS–2, the artificial planet, has a computer that may be able to provide you with useful information about the location of the galactic starship. Drakon, on Samelbub, is a Maglan pirate base, but there's also a Sondarian research station there.

TO CHECK MAP OF FEENAR, SEE PAGE 39.

TO CHECK MAP OF OS–2, SEE PAGE 43.

TO CHECK MAP OF SAMELBUB, SEE PAGE 19.

If you decide to head toward Feenar, turn to page 130.

If you decide to visit OS–2, turn to page 5.

If you travel to Samelbub instead, turn to page 26.

Dirn's vehicle, with you clinging to the back, hurtles down the corridor. After what seems like ages, you emerge into an enormous cavern, almost a world in itself. Directly in front of you on the shore of a broad lake is Narnk, a strange city of geometric shapes—blocks, cubes, and spheres. You see hundreds of people of the same race as Dirn. Although they're all ages and sizes, none is more than three feet high.

Following Dirn, you walk into the city. Most of the people ignore you, but a few stare at you in amazement. You wonder how many creatures from other worlds they've seen.

"It seems funny that there's so much water underground on this planet," you say. "The surface is all desert."

"Appearances are sometimes deceiving," Dirn says. "Every few million years, Alkon changes its orbit around the orange sun. Then there's heavy rainfall for a few hundred years, and the surface becomes covered with a tropical jungle. When the rains stop, the deserts return, but meanwhile, the water has drained down to these regions deep underground."

You stop in front of a building that towers over everything else in the city.

"This is the laboratory," Dirn says. "I must return to the entry port—but good luck on your search."

Before you can thank him, Dirn has already dashed away down a narrow street.

Turn to page 86.

You decide to avoid the cities of Klanton and search the frozen mountains that crisscross the planet.

You weave back and forth across an almost endless series of peaks, bringing your scoutcraft down close to any column of ice that could possibly be a starship in disguise. At night, you hide your ship in one of the many ice caves at the foot of the mountains.

After a few days of searching the icy wastes, spots are swimming in front of your eyes from the constant glare of the ice. You decide to refuel in Tantel and then head for Mazar.

TO CHECK MAP OF MAZAR, SEE PAGE 61.

Turn to page 60.

You thank Shind and follow the Klantonians to where the ice sled is parked. It's large and shaped like a boat.

The Western Mountains are one sheer vertical peak after another, but the Klantonians scale them with ease. To you, the sled ride feels a lot like being on a ten-thousand-foot roller coaster.

Finally, you reach the Sondarian research station, set high atop an ice mountain. The Klantonians stay parked nearby, chattering among themselves as you enter the door of the station.

Turn to page 108.

You find Torc as busy and as noisy as ever. You search all over the city, but you can't learn any news about the hidden galactic starship.

Discouraged, you head for a rest zone far across the city. It has a soundproof area where you can get a good meal and a good rest—and it's free for travelers.

You lose track of how long you sleep, but you wake up feeling thoroughly rested and ready to resume your quest. The matter transmitter available for visitors to Torc is a short-distance transmitter. It will take you only to the city of Tlar on Bazul, so you must continue your search there.

Turn to page 28.

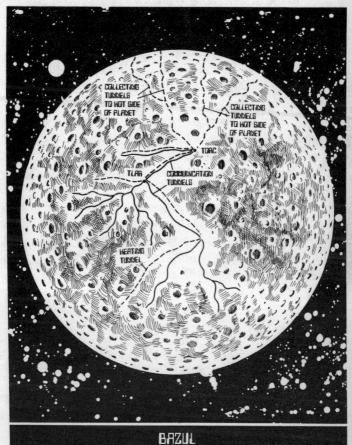

COLLECTING
TUNNELS
TO HOT SIDE
OF PLANET

COLLECTING
TUNNELS
TO HOT SIDE
OF PLANET

TOAC

TLAR

COMMUNICATION
TUNNELS

HEATING
TUNNEL

BAZUL
(DARK SIDE)

The warm-suit is a tight fit, but it's sturdy enough to keep you from freezing. You and Shind set out toward the city of Klar.

Just outside the city gate, a delegation of Klantonians comes to meet you. They look like small, round, fluffy balls of fur. A single eyestalk rises out of the top of each of their heads. You can't see if they have feet under the fur, but they glide with ease across the ice. When you reach them, they jabber excitedly with a series of high-pitched sounds. Shind is able to understand them and replies with a good imitation of their speech.

"I told them what you're looking for," Shind says. "They'll take you by sled into the Western Mountains, where the research station is located. I must leave you here to continue my work."

Turn to page 99.

You head down toward the now-familiar endless stretch of water. In some places, the ocean is shallow enough so that you can see the bottom through the crystal-clear water. You spend hours skimming just above the surface of your ship, looking for something that could be a submerged starship.

Finally, you decide to refuel on Aquar. While you're there, you study your map computer. It might be useful to visit the Sondarian research station on Mazar next. Or, you could try a completely different planet. The nearest ones are Bazul—and Tenopia, though you don't want to go there!

TO CHECK MAP OF MAZAR, SEE PAGE 61.

TO CHECK MAP OF BAZUL, SEE PAGE 101.

If you travel to the Sondarian Research Station on Mazar, turn to page 127.

If you travel to Bazul, turn to page 58.

"No, I don't have all the code words yet," you tell the robot.

"Then I suggest you leave now and come back when you do."

You can't get anything more out of the robot, and you don't see much point in consulting that strange computer again. Quickly, you head for the scoutcraft hangar.

The ship that you are given is equipped to carry extra fuel supplies—enough to take you to the opposite end of Star System Tenopia. It's a good opportunity to visit one of the planets that is farthest away from OS–2: Mazar or Alkon.

TO CHECK MAP OF MAZAR, SEE PAGE 61.

TO CHECK MAP OF ALKON, SEE PAGE 49.

If you decide to visit Mazar, turn to page 127.

If you decide to visit Alkon instead, turn to page 48.

The dense woods at the edge of the field are eerily silent. You tiptoe as quietly as you can. Suddenly, your foot catches on a wire, and you go sprawling on the ground. At the same time an alarm siren blasts from the roof of the building across the field. Searchlights pierce the darkness, catching you helpless in their beams. Too late, you realize you should have known that the pirates would have an alarm system set up to prevent anyone from sneaking up on the pirate base. Within seconds you are surrounded by six pirate guards.

They tie you up securely and put you on a pirate ship—one about to take off for their base at Drakon on the planet Samelbub.

Turn to page 85.

The scientist in charge of the research station is a Sondarian female. "What is it that I can help you with?" she asks briskly.

You tell her about your travels from planet to planet, looking for the galactic patrol starship and trying to piece together the code.

"The starship is not here," she says. "My instruments would tell me if it were on Klanton. And if it ever was here, it would have been found out and stolen by the Grivels by now. They will steal anything if given a chance. I know because they come from the polar regions of my own planet. As for the code, not all research stations have it, and those that do have been given only one part of it."

"Do you have it? Will you tell me what your part is?" you ask.

"The word *glass*," she answers. "Of course, you realize that in order to learn the correct order of the code words you will have to see the Council of Elders on Sondar."

"I feel as if I've been traveling in circles in an endless maze," you say.

Go on to the next page.

She smiles gently. "There is an end to your journey. If you have all five of the code words, I will tell you where to find the elders on Sondar. If you do not have all five words, I suggest you try Feenar next. The festival there attracts visitors from throughout the star system. You may even be able to discover the location of the starship. Either way, the Klantonians will take you back to your ship."

If you have all five code words,
turn to page 32.

If not, reclaim your scoutcraft and
turn to page 34.

The pilot emerges, a hominid dressed in a warm-suit. She is not more than three feet high. Hoping that the distress signal is not a trick, you wrap yourself in thermal blankets from your ship's emergency supplies and step outside your scoutcraft.

"I had to stop you," shouts the other pilot in the galactic language. "The heat from your scoutcraft would've damaged Klar, the ice city up ahead! Do you need help? I'm Shind, a scientist from the Federation of Alkon."

You introduce yourself and tell Shind about your quest.

"I think you want to visit the Sondarian research station here," she says. "First let me put together a warm-suit for you. You won't survive long in this sub-zero temperature without one. Then I'll bring you to the Klantonians. They'll take you the rest of the way by sled."

Turn to page 102.

You search Feenar thoroughly, stopping only to eat and sleep at night at the rest station. At last, you're forced to conclude that the galactic patrol's emergency starship is not hidden on Feenar. You head back toward the town of Varavam on Sondar to consult with Tanalia once again.

Turn to page 122.

You find a rest station not too far away where you're able to get fuel. Then you spend the day questioning everyone who comes through and speaks the galactic language.

Though you meet some interesting creatures, you don't learn anything useful about the hidden starship. You spend the evening in an automated rest cabin. As you pass through its doorway, sensors determine what kind of life-form you are and synthesize a delicious meal for you.

After you eat, you settle down in the cabin's comfortable bed. Early the next morning you check your map computer to determine where to go next. Samelbub and Alkon are the nearest planets. Of course, Samelbub contains the Maglan pirate base—but for that reason, you haven't explored it fully.

Both planets have Sondarian research stations, and you might pick up valuable information at one of them.

**TO CHECK MAP OF SAMELBUB,
SEE PAGE 19.**

**TO CHECK MAP OF ALKON,
SEE PAGE 49.**

If you decide to visit Samelbub, turn to page 26.

If you decide to visit Alkon, turn to page 48.

"You *have* acquired the code," says the same Sondarian elder. "Listen closely: If you number the words as you have given them, they are *one, two, three, four, five*. If you order them correctly to activate the starship, the order will be *three, one, five, four, two*."

You puzzle this out. *Arcs, glass, pelephin, liquid, over* . . . "Pelephin arcs over liquid glass!" you cry.

"Correct."

Tanalia, who had been conferring with one of the other elders, turns to you. "Now that you have the code," she says, "you must find the starship as soon as possible. It would be very dangerous for you to be captured. The elders have offered transmission of you *and* your craft to one of the three planets they consider most likely to contain the hidden ship: Alkon, Feenar, or Bazul."

TO CHECK MAP OF ALKON, SEE PAGE 49.

TO CHECK MAP OF FEENAR, SEE PAGE 39.

TO CHECK MAP OF BAZUL, SEE PAGE 101.

If you go to Alkon, turn to page 59.

If you go to Feenar, turn to page 111.

If you go to Bazul, turn to page 83.

The specialist probes your mind briefly, then smiles. "I see that you still remember the code word for this station; *liquid*. But you must know that we can offer you little further help in your search."

"Can you give me fuel?"

"Yes, we will be happy to do that."

She arranges for you to receive enough fuel to take you to the farthest reaches of the star system: Sondar, Klanton, or OS–2.

TO CHECK MAP OF SONDAR, SEE PAGE 77.

TO CHECK MAP OF KLANTON, SEE PAGE 81.

TO CHECK MAP OF OS–2, SEE PAGE 43.

If you decide to visit Sondar, turn to page 88.

If you travel to Klanton, the ice planet, turn to page 118.

If you visit OS–2, the artificial planet, turn to page 5.

You regain consciousness inside the saucer-shaped spaceship. Several small hominids are watching you closely. You learn, to your relief, that they understand the galactic language. You also learn that they are Grivels, that they inhabit Sondar's polar regions, and that they—and you—are headed for Sondar.

"What were you doing among the Klantonians?" one of the Grivels asks.

"I'm looking for a starship so that I can get back to my own planet, Earth."

"Klanton seems an unlikely place to be looking for a starship," the Grivel says. "And the Klantonians! Nasty little creatures they are—have a fierce bite. We've been at war with them for hundreds of years."

"They don't look like they can fight anyone. All they have is ice," you say.

"You'd be surprised at what they can do with it. They can make supercooled ice that's as hard as steel," says the Grivel. "Anyway, we had to get you out of there before you got killed. When we get to Sondar, we'll give you a scoutcraft so you can continue your search."

Go on to the next page.

Soon you arrive at the Grivels' polar-cap headquarters on Sondar. They furnish you with a scoutcraft. You thank them and take off, flying south toward Kornik and the warmer areas of Sondar.

**TO CHECK MAP OF SONDAR,
SEE PAGE 77.**

Turn to page 88.

As you approach Klanton the planet looks like a milky white marble floating in space.

If you've visited the city of Klar before, turn to page 95. If not, read on . . .

When you get closer, you can see a city rising majestically in the distance, its tall, pointed spires carved out of glistening ice. As you fly toward the city you see a scoutcraft resting on the frozen surface below. Its lights are blinking the signal for an SOS. You land nearby.

Turn to page 110.

The Sondarians in Tamsung are friendly enough but can do little to help you. They don't have a scoutcraft to offer you this time. You must continue to travel by matter transmitter for now.

The transmitter in Tamsung can send you to either Feenar, the park planet, or Bazul, the planet closest to the orange sun.

**TO CHECK MAP OF FEENAR,
SEE PAGE 39.**

**TO CHECK MAP OF BAZUL,
SEE PAGE 101.**

*If you decide to travel to Feenar,
turn to page 54.*

If you go to Bazul instead, turn to page 56.

The Sondarians of Kornik greet you warmly. This time, they bring you to their governor—a stout, light-haired hominid with the Sondarians' usual look of intelligence.

The governor eyes you sternly. "Best tell the truth, for the Council of Elders will test you when you stand before them. Have you acquired the code?" he asks. "If not, I suggest you step into the matter transmitter."

If you say yes, turn to page 32.

If you say no, turn to page 125.

Tanalia greets you with a shout. "You have not found the starship yet?"

You shake your head, and she sighs. "Every minute, the danger grows," she warns you. "If the Maglan pirates were to capture you and learn the code . . ." She leaves the sentence unfinished.

"Can the elders help me?"

"They already have: they've imported a supply of fuel for you. Now you must search another of the possible planets where the starship might be hidden: Alkon or Feenar or Bazul."

"Thank you, Tanalia." You check your computer maps, thinking hard.

TO CHECK MAP OF ALKON, SEE PAGE 49.

TO CHECK MAP OF FEENAR, SEE PAGE 39.

TO CHECK MAP OF BAZUL, SEE PAGE 101.

If you go to Alkon, turn to page 59.

If you go to Feenar, turn to page 111.

If you go to Bazul, turn to page 45.

You sit down at the control panel. You think for a moment, trying to be sure of the order of words that the Council of Elders gave you. "Pelephin arcs over liquid glass," you say at last.

"Welcome to Automatic Starship Cassiopeia," replies a mechanical voice. "The ship awaits your order."

"To Earth!" you say excitedly. "Let's go!"

Congratulations! At last you've escaped from Star System Tenopia. There's a slight vibration as the starship rises smoothly into the Bazulian sky. You find a space hammock and settle back to enjoy the ride.

The End

You step inside the matter-transmitter booth, and a moment later you find yourself in a large glass case. You are closed in on all sides. Outside the case, bending over it, is a huge creature, twelve feet high at least. You can hear its deep, muffled voice through the thick glass.

"I've caught another one trying to transmit," the creature says.

"Another one!" says an even deeper voice.

A second creature, this one even larger than the first, stares at you through the glass.

"You'd better let it go before we get into trouble," it says.

"But I just caught it!" the first one protests.

The two creatures continue to argue. Finally, the smaller one opens the top of the glass case. A huge tentacle reaches in and wraps itself around your body. You are lifted out of the case and carried a long way to an outside door of the building you are in, and thrown out. The enormous door slams shut behind you.

Turn to page 54.

In the prison, you find that Jarn still has his escape transmitter working. Fortunately, the pirates haven't caught on to it yet. You have to wait until a full week has passed since the last prisoner escaped. Then, Jarn wishes you luck, and you step into the shower stall where the matter transmitter is hidden.

Turn to page 74.

As you fly over the waters of Mazar you see below you what must be the Sondarian research station. It looks more like a large egg than the tower shown on your computer map. But its location matches up with your map, and it's the only structure of any sort for miles.

The scoutcraft hovers near the top of the egg as you look for an entrance. The sides of the egg are perfectly smooth; there's no sign of any door or window or even of a radar device.

You decide to send a message in the galactic language explaining your search. You transmit the message three times. There's no response from the egg.

If you've visited the Sondarian Research Station on Mazar before, turn to page 41. If not, read on . . .

Discouraged, you decide to chart a new course. You've just taken out your pocket computer when you hear the sound of chimes. You look up from your computer to see the egg opening into petal-shaped sections that spread out on the water like a large, white lily.

"You may now land," says a voice inside your head. And before you can even touch the controls, the scoutcraft lands in the very center of the flower.

Turn to page 131.

Inside the Sondarian research station on Alkon you are greeted by the chief specialist in aliens. Except for her pointed ears, she looks very much like an Earthling.

If you've been to the Sondarian Research Station on Alkon before, turn to page 115. If not, read on . . .

You tell her about your search for the galactic patrol starship and the code that will activate it.

"There are many searching for that ship," the Sondarian says. "Will you allow me to probe your mind, so that I can be sure you are not an agent of the Maglan pirates?"

You agree and feel a brief tickling sensation run through you.

She appears satisfied. "You know Jarn," she says. "He has been a good friend to my people. So I will tell you that I do not think the starship is on this planet. In fact, I am not sure that any Sondarian knows its location. That information you may have to get from an entirely different source. However, once you have all parts of the code, the Sondarian Council of Elders will help you to order it properly."

Go on to the next page.

"Has this station been given a code word?" you ask.

She smiles. "Yes. A strange word since there is not much of it here on the desert planet—*liquid*. Now, if you have all five parts of the code, I will send you to the Council of Elders on Sondar. Otherwise, I suggest you try another planet—perhaps Klanton."

"I don't have enough fuel to get to Klanton or Sondar," you tell her.

"The Alkonians will take care of that," she assures you. "Now which will it be? Do you have the five code words?"

If you say yes, turn to page 32.

If you say no, turn to page 80.

The flight from Klanton is long and uneventful, but finally you land beside an emerald-green lake in Feenar. As you walk toward the shore you smile—it's great to be in a warm climate again!

Nearby is a small pavilion that serves as a guest house. You introduce yourself to the guests and ask about the galactic starship, but no one's even heard of it.

You return to your scoutcraft only to find that you're almost out of fuel! You will have to either find fuel close by or explore Feenar on foot.

 TO CHECK MAP OF FEENAR, SEE PAGE 39.

If you look for fuel, turn to page 113.

If you set off on foot to explore Feenar, turn to page 54.

A male Sondarian, who looks to be about your age, greets you. "Do not be alarmed," says the voice inside your head. "I can exchange thoughts directly with your mind."

"What about the galactic patrol starship?" you ask silently. "Can you tell me where it is, or give me any of the code?"

"The code only," comes the reply. "The word I give you is *pelephin*."

"Pelephin?" you say aloud in surprise. "That's the symbol on the key to the starship."

"I know nothing about the starship," says the Sondarian's voice inside your head. "Do you have all five words of the code? If not, I suggest you continue your search on Klanton."

If you answer yes, turn to page 32.

If you answer no, turn to page 5.

ABOUT THE CREATOR

EDWARD PACKARD is a graduate of Princeton University and Columbia Law School. He is the creator of Bantam's Escape™ and Choose Your Own Adventure® series and the author of many books for children.

ABOUT THE AUTHOR

RICHARD BRIGHTFIELD is a graduate of Johns Hopkins University, where he studied biology, psychology, and archaeology. For many years he worked as a graphic designer at Columbia University. He has written *The Deadly Shadow, Secret of the Pyramids, The Curse of Batterslea Hall, The Phantom Submarine, The Dragons' Den,* and *The Secret Treasure of Tibet* in the Choose Your Own Adventure® series and *Trapped in the Sea Kingdom* and *Terror on Kabran* in the Escape™ from Tenopia series. He has also coauthored more than a dozen game books with his wife, Glory. The Brightfields and their daughter, Savitri, live in Gardiner, New York.

ABOUT THE ILLUSTRATOR

DAVID PERRY studied art in New York and Rome. He has written and illustrated a book for children, *The Grox and Eugene,* in addition to illustrating books and periodicals.

CHOOSE YOUR OWN ADVENTURE

BLAST INTO THE PAST!

TIME MACHINE

Each of these books is a time machine and you are at the controls . . .

☐	23601	**SECRETS OF THE KNIGHTS #1**	$1.95
		J. Gasperini	
☐	25399	**SEARCH FOR DINOSAURS #2**	$2.25
		D. Bischoff	
☐	25619	**SWORD OF THE SAMURAI #3**	$2.25
		M. Reaves & S. Perry	
☐	25616	**SAIL WITH PIRATES #4**	$2.25
		J. Gasperini	
☐	25606	**CIVIL WAR SECRET AGENT #5**	$2.25
		Steve Perry	
☐	25797	**THE RINGS OF SATURN #6**	$2.25
		Arthur Cover	
☐	24722	**ICE AGE EXPLORER #7**	$1.95
		Dougal Dixon	
☐	25073	**THE MYSTERY OF ATLANTIS #8**	$2.25
		Jim Gasperini	
☐	25180	**WILD WEST RIDER #9**	$2.25
		Stephen Overholser	
☐	25300	**AMERICAN REVOLUTIONARY #10**	$2.25
		Arthur Byron	
☐	25431	**MISSION TO WORLD WAR II #11**	$2.25
		S. Nanus & M. Kornblatt	
☐	25538	**SEARCH FOR THE NILE #12**	$2.25
		Robert W. Walker	

Prices and availability subject to change without notice.

Buy them at your local bookstore or use this handy coupon for ordering: